NICK JR The BACKYARDIGANS
Music Player
Storybook™

written by **Christine Ricci**
illustrated by **Jason Fruchter**
based on the original teleplays by
Janice Burgess, Adam Peltzman, McPaul Smith
and Radha Blank

Contents

Reader's Digest
Children's Books™

Pleasantville, New York • Montréal, Québec • Bath, United Kingdom

Princess CleoTasha

Play Song 1

Once upon a time there was a princess. "I'm not just any princess. I am Princess CleoTasha from ancient Egypt," said the princess. "Where are my servants?" Servants Austin, Tyrone, and Pablo ran up to Princess CleoTasha and bowed. "Here we are, your highness."

The servants were always fulfilling the princess' demands. When she was hot, they fanned her. When she was hungry, they brought her sandwiches. When she was thirsty, they brought her water. Unfortunately, the princess never said, "please" or "thank you."

4

Play Song 2

One day, the princess wanted to be taken to her palace on the banks of the deep, green, River Nile. But when they arrived, it was hot and dusty, the garden was wilted, and the River Nile was dry land. Princess CleoTasha was very unhappy.

"Fill up the river!" she ordered.

"Only you can fill the river with water," replied Servant Tyrone. "You need to learn the secret of the Nile." The servants told Princess CleoTasha that if she brought three very special presents to Sphinx Uniqua, the Sphinx would reveal the secret. Reluctantly, Princess CleoTasha agreed to find the presents and visit Sphinx Uniqua.

Play Song 3

First, they had to find the Jewel of the Waters. They weren't on the road very long when Princess CleoTasha became hot. "Let's stop here! I need to be fanned."

Servant Tyrone waved a large fan up and down to give the princess air. The fan was quite heavy and Servant Tyrone was so tired from the journey that he leaned against a wall—an invisible wall with a secret door that opened to reveal hundreds of sparkling jewels!

"Wow, look at all these incredible jewels!" the princess said. She wanted to keep all the jewels for herself, but she could only take the Jewel of the Waters. Otherwise, she wouldn't be told the secret of the Nile. "Find me the jewel," she ordered. Servant Tyrone pointed it out to her.

"I found the Jewel of the Waters!" Princess CleoTasha declared. "It's heavy! You carry it." She tossed the jewel to her loyal servant.

Servants Pablo and Austin asked if Servant Tyrone had helped the Princess find the jewel. "Yeah," nodded Servant Tyrone. "But you know Princess CleoTasha. She never says, 'please' or 'thank you.'"

Play Song 4 The second present was a yellow lotus flower from the top of the Cliffs of Karnak. The only way to the top was to walk up a very long flight of stairs. Princess CleoTasha hadn't climbed very many stairs when she grew tired and insisted that Servant Pablo carry her to the top. Of course, she did not say, "please." And when Servant Pablo got the princess to the top, she did not say, "thank you" either.

On the cliff top, the princess saw many beautiful flowers. She was about to pick some red and blue ones for herself when Servant Pablo reminded her that she could only pick one yellow flower as a gift to the Sphinx. "If you touch any other flower, you will not be told the secret."

"Oh, for goodness sakes," said the princess. "Where is this yellow flower?"

Servant Pablo helped Princess CleoTasha find the flower. "I have found the second present for the Sphinx!" she exclaimed, as she handed the flower to her servant.

"Princess CleoTasha never says, 'please' or 'thank you,'" Servant Pablo grumbled as he trudged down the stairs.

"What's the last present?" Princess CleoTasha asked.

Servant Austin told her it was water from the Secret Oasis. When they arrived at the oasis, they saw a crystal blue pool of water.

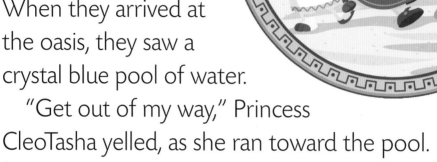

"Get out of my way," Princess CleoTasha yelled, as she ran toward the pool. "I'm so thirsty!"

"No, Princess!" Servant Austin shouted. "You cannot drink the water of the Secret Oasis! Only the Sphinx can drink it. You have to bring a cup of this water to the Sphinx."

Play Song 5

But none of the servants had a cup. "Well, how am I supposed to carry water without a cup?" complained Princess CleoTasha.

"You could use a curled leaf," suggested Servant Austin, and he handed her a leaf curled into a cup shape. Princess CleoTasha took it and filled it with water. "You carry it!" she muttered, as she handed it to Servant Austin. "Don't spill any!" And with that, she walked away.

Servant Austin turned to the other servants, "That Princess CleoTasha never says, 'please' or 'thank you.'"

"We know," they replied, as they gathered up the Sphinx's presents.

Play Song 6

"Greetings, O Sphinx Uniqua," Princess CleoTasha called out, as she and the servants approached the Sphinx. "I have brought you three presents so I can learn the secret that will fill the Nile River."

"I love presents," giggled Sphinx Uniqua. Princess CleoTasha gave her the three gifts.

"Very good," praised Sphinx Uniqua. "Getting these presents must have taken a lot of hard work," said Sphinx Uniqua. "Have you thanked your servants for all their help?"

"Well...no," the princess mumbled. Then the Sphinx leaned forward and whispered the secret of the Nile into Princess CleoTasha's ear.

"Oh, for goodness sakes," exclaimed the princess. Turning to her servants, the princess said, "Thank you for helping me find the gifts and for being such wonderful servants."

The servants were shocked. The princess had never, ever thanked them. Suddenly, they noticed that the Nile River was filling with water!

Then Sphinx Uniqua repeated the secret for everyone to hear. "The secret of the Nile—the secret to almost anything—is to always say 'please' and 'thank you.'"

"That reminds me, O Sphinx," Princess CleoTasha said. "Thank you for telling me the secret!" Then she turned to her servants. "Please come back to the palace and I'll get you a snack!" And they all happily returned to the palace.

Monster Detectives

Play Song 1

"I'm the Soccer Monster! Bleh! Bleh!" shouted Pablo. "Soccer Monsters love soccer!" Pablo the Soccer Monster stomped over to a pink-spotted soccer ball lying next to a sandbox. He kicked the ball back and forth. "Soccer Monsters love soccer balls!" The Soccer Monster decided to play with the ball at his Soccer Monster Castle. But as excited as he was to find the pink-spotted soccer ball, he was also a little lonely. "I just wish there was another Soccer Monster to play soccer with me."

Nearby, Detective Tyrone was always ready to help solve a mystery. Suddenly, he heard someone cry for help. "Detective Tyrone, on the case! What seems to be the problem?"

"Help!" cried Uniqua. "I lost my soccer ball." Detective Tyrone took out his notepad. "Tell me what happened."

"Well," began Uniqua. "I left my favorite pink-spotted soccer ball here when I went inside. And when I came out, my soccer ball was gone!"

"Young lady, it sounds like this is a case of a missing soccer ball," said Detective Tyrone. "I better investigate." Detective Tyrone pulled out his magnifying glass and searched the backyard. He examined the grass, circled the sandbox, and looked for any trace of the ball in the bushes. He didn't find the soccer ball. But he did find some interesting footprints.

Play Song 3

"Young lady, your soccer ball has been stolen by the Soccer Monster!" exclaimed Detective Tyrone. "I'll go to the Soccer Monster Castle and get your ball back! You stay here."

But Uniqua wanted to go to the castle, too. Detective Tyrone agreed to let her go only if she would obey the Monster Detective Rules. Rule Number One was that she had to be very quiet and sneaky. Rule Number Two was that she could not play soccer with the Soccer Monster. If she did, she would become a Soccer Monster, too! Uniqua thought that becoming a Soccer Monster would be pretty neat, but she agreed to obey the rules.

Play Song 4

Detective Tyrone led Uniqua to the Soccer Monster Castle. The door creaked open and they walked inside. Quietly, they wandered through the rooms of the castle looking for the pink-spotted soccer ball. "The Soccer Monster really likes soccer," observed Uniqua as she examined the soccer pictures and trophies in each room. But the castle was old and dusty and Uniqua was allergic to dust. Dust made her sneeze! "Aa...Aaa...Aaaaa...ACHOO!"

The sneeze echoed through the castle. Uh-oh! Uniqua's sneeze wasn't quiet! Uniqua had broken Rule Number One!

Meanwhile, the Soccer Monster was playing soccer by himself in his secret soccer gym. As he kicked the ball toward the net, he was suddenly interrupted by a very loud sneeze coming from somewhere in his castle!

"Bleh! Someone's in my castle," grumbled the Soccer Monster. He ran through the castle to find out who it was.

Detective Tyrone and Uniqua were wandering through the castle when they came upon a hidden door. The door led into a secret soccer gym filled with soccer balls.

Play Song 5

I bet my soccer ball is in here somewhere, thought Uniqua as she looked for her special ball with pink spots.

Just then, she heard, "Soccerrr!" Uniqua looked up and saw her soccer ball. But it wasn't Detective Tyrone who had found her ball. It was the Soccer Monster!

"Please play soccer with me," said the Soccer Monster. He kicked the ball to Uniqua and she gladly passed the ball back.

Suddenly, there was a POOF! Uniqua turned into a Soccer Monster.

"Hey! Being a Soccer Monster is great," Uniqua said with a giggle, and she and Soccer Monster Pablo began a soccer game.

Detective Tyrone was very nervous. Rule Number Two had been broken. Uniqua had played soccer with the Soccer Monster and now there were two Soccer Monsters. "Stop the game!" interrupted Detective Tyrone.

Play Song 6

"It seems this case is solved. My detective duties are done. Being a Soccer Monster looks like fun. What do I have to do to become a Soccer Monster?"

"Play soccer with us!" cheered the Soccer Monsters. So Tyrone kicked the ball to Pablo, who kicked it to Uniqua, and then she kicked it back to Tyrone. POOF! Detective Tyrone became a Soccer Monster, too.

The three Soccer Monsters decided to make up their own rules. Rule Number One was to play soccer! Rule Number Two was when they got hungry, have a snack! So the Soccer Monster friends played soccer all afternoon, stopping only for delicious snacks!

Pirate Treasure

Play Song 1 "Arrr!" said Uniqua as she looked through her telescope. "I'm Captain Uniqua, the patch-eyed pirate! You can tell I'm a pirate because I say, 'Arrr!'"

"Arrr!" replied Captain Austin. "I'm a pirate too—a pirate with a hook for a hand!" Suddenly Captain Uniqua saw something in the sandbox. It was half of a pirate treasure map!

"Only half of a map?" asked Captain Austin. "Too bad we don't have the whole map."

"Half of a map is better than nothing!" said Captain Uniqua. "Come on, matey! Let's go find the treasure." Captains Uniqua and Austin climbed aboard their pirate ship and sailed off on their quest for pirate treasure.

Play Song 2

Soon after, Tyrone and Pablo walked over to the sandbox. As they dug in the sand, Pablo's shovel uncovered half of a pirate treasure map.

"Too bad it's not the whole map," said Tyrone.

"But half a map is better than nothing," replied Pablo. "Let's be pirates and look for the treasure! I'll be Captain Pablo. Arrr!"

"I'll be Captain Tyrone," said Tyrone. "Arrr!"

Captains Tyrone and Pablo took their half of the treasure map, climbed aboard their pirate ship, and set sail for the high seas!

Captains Pablo and Tyrone spotted the other pirate ship in the distance. They quietly sailed their boat next to the ship and secretly climbed aboard. "Arrr! We're raiding your ship, you scurvy pirates," said Captain Pablo.

"Arrr! Well, we're defending our ship, you scurvy pirates!" Captain Austin returned.

"Arrr!"

"Arrr!" The pirates said, "Arrr!" at each other as they tried to raid and defend the ship.

"Arrrrr! We win!" cheered Captain Tyrone. "And that means that Captains Uniqua and Austin have to walk to the end of the plank and splash into the water!"

"Hey! That sounds like fun," said Captain Pablo. "Maybe WE should walk the plank."

"Uh-uh," said Captain Uniqua. "YOU won the raid, so WE get to walk the plank."

Play
Song
3

Captains Uniqua and Austin climbed up on the plank, and walked forward until they got to the very end. Then they jumped. But instead of splashing into the water, they landed in the soft, warm sand of a desert island—a desert island just like the map said they needed to find. Excited, the pirates ran down the beach in search of treasure.

"Come on, matey," Captain Pablo said to Captain Tyrone as they jumped out of the boat. "We can use our half of the map to find the treasure!"

After walking for a long time without finding any treasure, Captains Pablo and Tyrone stopped to check their half of the map. Captains Austin and Uniqua were studying their own half of the map when they bumped right into the other pirates. The two maps went flying and landed side by side on the desert sand, making one map. In the middle of this map, an X marked the spot where the treasure was buried. Knowing that they needed both halves of the map to find the treasure, the pirates agreed to work together to look for the X.

Play Song 4

The first mark they came to was a T. Then they came to a U, and a V, and finally a W. "No one would bury treasure under a T, U, V, or W," said Captain Uniqua.

"Yeah, only X marks the spot," said Captain Tyrone. "Let's keep looking!"

The next mark they came to was the X.

"All right, mateys! Let's dig for treasure!" exclaimed Captain Austin.

Each of the pirates grabbed a shovel and began to dig. Before long, Captain Uniqua's shovel hit something in the sand. It was the treasure chest!

Play Song 5 Inside the treasure chest was the biggest and most beautiful diamond in the entire world.

"We're rich!" exclaimed Captain Tyrone.

But Captain Pablo was worried. "What if other pirates try to raid us to capture our diamond? Maybe we should hide our treasure."

The pirates thought Captain Pablo might be right. After all, pirates are known for raids. They decided to bury the treasure again. But as soon as the treasure was buried, Captain Pablo started to pace back and forth across the sand. "Oh, no! I've forgotten where we buried it. Where is the treasure?"

"We buried it right here," said Captain Tyrone, pointing at the sand.

Play Song 6

"Oh yeah," said Captain Pablo. "Maybe we should mark the spot so we won't forget where it is."

"We could use an X to mark the spot," suggested Captain Uniqua.

But somehow using an X didn't seem quite right since all pirates used X to mark the spot. The pirates wanted to be trickier. They wanted to mark their spot with something that no one would ever think to look under. The pirates thought...and thought...and thought. All of a sudden, it came to them. They marked their treasure spot with a Y.

"What a pirate-y adventure!" exclaimed the pirate friends as they set sail for home.

The Snow Fort

 "It's a perfect day for a snowy adventure," said Tyrone. "I'm Mountie Tyrone!"

"And I'm Mountie Pablo!" said Pablo as he gave Tyrone the special Mountie salute.

"A Mountie's duty is to protect the Mountie Snow Fort way up north in the rugged Yukon," Tyrone explained.

"Mounties on duty!" chanted Tyrone and Pablo as they started the long march through the snow toward the Mountie Snow Fort.

Play Song 2

When Mountie Tyrone and Mountie Pablo reached the Mountie Snow Fort, they opened the giant vault with the world's biggest snowball inside.

"It's our duty to protect the Snow Fort and the world's biggest snowball from Snow Fort raiders!" exclaimed Mountie Tyrone. The Mounties closed the vault with a *CLANG* and began guarding the world's biggest snowball.

Uniqua and Tasha also thought it was a perfect day for exploring the snowy Yukon. "I'm a ski patroller!" said Uniqua. "Ski patrollers ski through the snow looking for people who need rescuing."

"Yup!" agreed Tasha. "We save them and then we give them delicious hot chocolate to warm them up!" Ski Patrollers Uniqua and Tasha checked their rescue equipment to make sure that they had their shovels, ice suction cups, and snow hooks. "And don't forget about our delectable hot chocolate," said Ski Patroller Tasha.

"Ski Patrol to the rescue!" they shouted as they skied off searching for people in trouble.

Play Song 3

After a little while, Ski Patroller Tasha grew tired. "There's no one around who needs rescuing! Maybe we should just give up and drink this scrumptious hot chocolate."

"We can't give up until we find someone to rescue!" said Ski Patroller Uniqua. "The Ski Patrol never gives up!"

Suddenly they heard a loud CLANG coming from a snow fort.

"It sounds like someone needs our help!" exclaimed Ski Patroller Uniqua.

"Ski Patrol to the rescue!" they cheered as they started skiing toward the Snow Fort.

Meanwhile, Mountie Pablo was on guard duty. He marched back and forth looking for Snow Fort invaders and snowball raiders. Suddenly, he saw two skiers approaching the fort. "Uh-oh! Look! Raiders!" shouted Mountie Pablo. "They've come to take the snowball!! Call the Mounties!"

"Pablo! Pablo! We are the Mounties," replied Mountie Tyrone. "And it's up to us to protect the world's biggest snowball!"

"But...but how? How do we protect it?" Mountie Pablo asked.

"Booby traps!" whispered Mountie Tyrone.

Play Song 4

Mounties Pablo and Tyrone's first booby trap would turn the stairs into a slippery ramp. Their second booby trap, would drop piles of snowballs to block the door. The Mounties' last booby trap would make snow blocks come out of the walls.

"Do you think our booby traps will work?" Mountie Pablo asked quietly.

"There's only one way to find out," answered Tyrone. "We have to go down and look around." Moutie Tyrone threw a rope ladder out the second-floor window, and the two mounties climbed down to the ground.

Ski Patrollers Tasha and Uniqua were determined to rescue whoever was inside the Snow Fort, but it was very tough. First, the stairs turned into an icy ramp, so they had to use their ice suction cups to climb up to the door.

Play
Song
5

Then a pile of snowballs fell on top of them and blocked the door. Luckily, they had their snow hooks. They climbed out of the snow pile and up the wall. But it got even harder! Large snow blocks came out of the wall, knocking the ski patrollers to the ground.

"We will not give up!" exclaimed Ski Patroller Uniqua. "Someone in that fort needs our help!"

"Well, we could always dig our way inside," said Ski Patroller Tasha. They took their shovels and dug through the snow until they finally were inside the Snow Fort. The two ski patrollers headed up to the second floor searching for people to rescue.

Play Song 6 Meanwhile, Mounties Tyrone and Pablo started back up the ladder, having not seen any raiders outside the fort. But as the Mounties reached the second-floor window, they came face to face with the Ski Patrol! Mounties Tyrone and Pablo were so surprised that they fell off the ladder and tumbled headfirst into the snow! "Help! Help!" they cried.

"Ski Patrol to the rescue!" chanted the Ski Patrollers as they ran over to rescue Mounties Tyrone and Pablo.

"We saved you!"
Ski Patroller Uniqua
said proudly as
she pulled the
Mounties out of
the snow.

"Would you care
for some tasty hot
chocolate to warm
you up?" offered Ski
Patroller Tasha.

Ski Patrollers and Mounties
alike shared the hot chocolate and they all agreed
that it was absolutely delicious!

"Well," said Mountie Tyrone. "That was an
excellent Yukon adventure, don't you think?"